W9-AGH-291

Now It Is Morning

Candace Whitman

Farrar Straus Giroux   New York

For my parents

Distributed in Canada by Douglas & McIntyre Ltd.
Color separations by Hong Kong Scanner Arts
Printed in Mexico
Typography by Filomena Tuosto
First edition, 1999

Library of Congress Cataloging-in-Publication Data
Whitman, Candace, date.
    Now it is morning / Candace Whitman.
        p.   cm.
    Summary: Morning comes to the farm, the town, and the city,
bringing different new-day noises, different ways of greeting the sun,
and different things to do in beginning a brand-new day.
    ISBN 0-374-35527-4
    [1. Morning—Fiction.]   I. Title.
PZ7.W5918No   1998
[E]—dc21   98-17120

Now it is morning. The sun is coming up.
It's a brand-new day on the farm.

The rooster crows with the dawn.

COCK-A-DOODLE-DO! COCK-A-DOODLE-DO!

The children come out to do their chores,
first lifting the latch on the big barn doors.

The cows low very loud. MOOOOO!

The chickens are fed,
and the horses get hay.

Then eggs are brought in for breakfast.

Now it is morning way down the road.
It's a brand-new day in the town.

Families are sleeping, but not for long.

The alarm says it's time to wake up.
BZZZZZ!

Dad calls to the children and lets the dog out.

Mom makes breakfast for all.

The children get ready for school.
They mustn't be late!

The bus comes at twenty-five past.

Now it is morning over the bridge.
It's a brand-new day in the city.

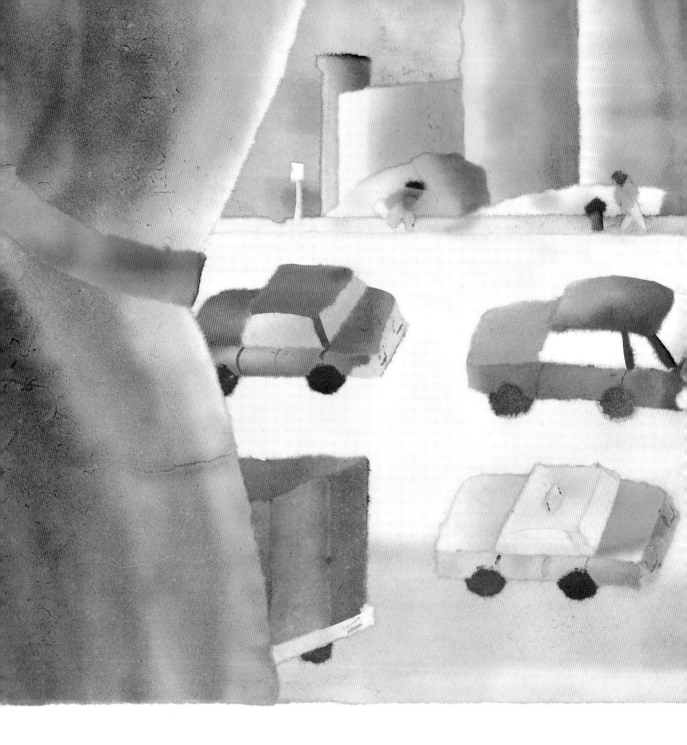

The cars outside make a great, wide river,

roaring with new-day noise.
VROOOM! VROOOM!

A little bit later, the old elevator stops

and the sitter steps out. GOOD MORNING!

Mommy leaves for work.
Soon it will be time to go . . .

to the park where the children play.

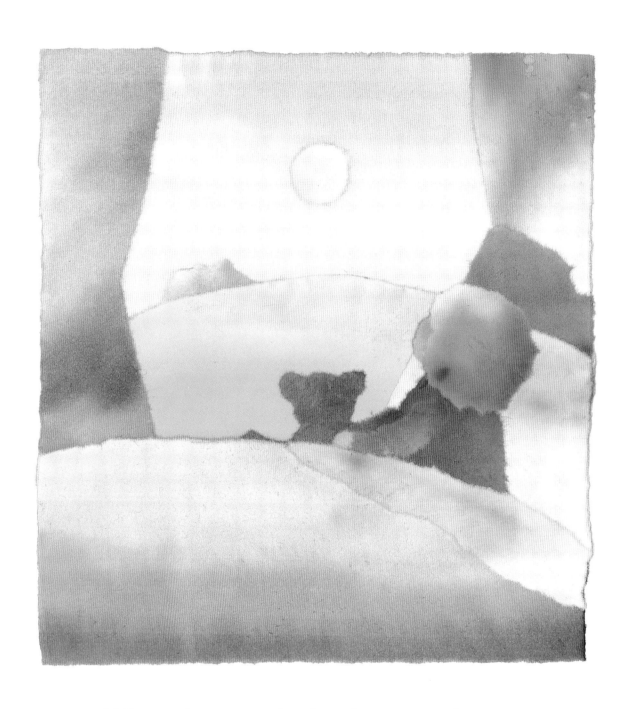

What do you do in the morning?